Dancing in My Bones

La Daans daan Mii Zoo

by
Wilfred Burton and Anne Patton

Translated by
Norman Fleury

Illustrated by
Sherry Farrell Racette

Library and Archives Canada Cataloguing in Publication

Burton, Wilfred, 1958-
 Dancing in my bones = La daans daan mii zoo / by Wilfred Burton
and Anne Patton ; illustrated by Sherry Farrell Racette ; Michif translation by
Norman Fleury.

Text in English and Michif-Cree.
ISBN 978-0-920915-89-9

 1. Métis--Juvenile fiction. I. Patton, Anne, 1942- II. Racette, Sherry Farrell
III. Fleury, Norman IV. Gabriel Dumont Institute of Native Studies and Applied
Research V. Title. VI. Title: Daans daan mii zoo.

PS8603.U78D36 2009   jC813'.6   C2009-902393-8

David Morin, Gabriel Dumont Institute Project Leader and Graphic Design
Darren Préfontaine, Gabriel Dumont Institute Editor
Karon Shmon, Gabriel Dumont Institute Publishing Coordinator

Printing: Globe Printers, Saskatoon, SK

Gabriel Dumont Institute
2—604 22nd Street West
Saskatoon, SK S7M 5W1
www.gdins.org
www.metismuseum.ca

The Gabriel Dumont Institute acknowledges the financial support of the Government of Canada and the Department of Canadian Heritage, which was used to publish this book.

Dancing in My Bones

La Daans daan Mii Zoo

Author Dedication

To all children who are willing to try
new things even if they're a little scared.

Snow swirled across the windshield as Nolin and Moushoom drove down the Midnight Lake road.
La niigh kii waashakayashew disseu la vitr aen pimbishoochik Nolin pi Mooshoom disseu li shmaen di laak maenwii.

When they passed the community hall, Nolin noticed there were no cars in front. Last night, people had driven for miles to enjoy New Year's Eve together.

Ka kawpishkawkik la hall, Nolin wawpatum ayka lii aatamoobil aan navaan la hall aen aayapiyit. Yayr a swayr, waayow ooschi li moond kii aen nakishkatochik poor li zhoor di laan.

Nolin remembered how Moushoom had danced. This morning Nolin practised the fancy jig steps with Moushoom until he knew them. Now Moushoom was driving Nolin home to Meadow Lake.

Nolin kishkishew taanshi Mooshoom ka ki niimit. A maatin Nolin ki koochi niimew lii boo stepp di jig avik Mooshoom zheusk a taan aen kishkaytuk lii stepp. Mooshoom kiiwaytahew Nolin a Meadow Lake.

"Do you think Uncle Bunny and Auntie Gigi will be at my house?" asked Nolin. "Will Uncle Bunny bring his fiddle? Will there be dancing?"

Moushoom nodded. "Lots of dancing, my boy. Us Michif like to start off the New Year happy." He winked at Nolin. "And our surprise'll make your mom real happy, too."

Nolin stared out the window, biting his lip. What if he couldn't remember the steps?

"Ki itayhten chiin moon nook Bunny pi ma taant Gigi chi ayaachik niikinaak?" itwew Nolin. "Ka paytow chiin soon vyaeloon moon nook Bunny? Ka niimiwuk chiin?"

Mooshoom nanamishkwayyiw, "Ka kishchi nimiwuk, moon pchi gaarsoon. Niiyanaan lii Michif ni maachistanaan li zhoor di laan aen chikaytamaak." Chiipihkwayshtawew Nolin, "Ki Maamaan ka kooshkwaytum pi ka chiihkaytum miina."

Nolin daan li chaassii aapanapew, pi sii baabinn taakwatum, kaykway kiishpin sii stepp waanikaychi?

The old green half-ton turned onto the highway. "Oyhoy!
It's really blowing now," exclaimed Moushoom. "Good thing my ol'
clunker knows the way to Meadow Lake." He peered through the
windshield. "Do you know what this snow reminds me of?"
Nolin forgot his worry. "Tell me, Moushoom!"

Li vyeu trukk vayr kii waashkiiw sur li shmaen. "Oyhoy!
Kishchi miishpoon aykwa," itwew Mooshoom. Enn chaans moon vyeu
truck kishkaytum taanday Meadow Lake. Aapanapew daan la vitr.
"Ki kishkayten chiin taanshi aen itaymuk awa la niigh."
Nolin noo ayiwawk kii koshtum. "Achimoo Mooshoom!"

"Well, me and my dad were driving this highway. I was just a bit bigger than you are now." After a while, Moushoom pointed to a narrow cutline drifted in with snow. "We spotted fresh moose tracks going down that line."

Nolin looked out the window. He couldn't see anything but blowing snow.

"Aa baen, ni paapaa aykwa niiya gii pimbishoonaan ooma li shmaen. Apishiish nawatch gii mishikitin aashphiishchi kiya ooma." Mooshoom itwahum iita la niigh ka ki piiwuhk daan li bwaa. "Gii maatahananik lii zaariyaanl daan la liing taykay."

Nolin paashpapew daan la vitr ooshchi. Maakaykwey waapahtum la niigh piiko aen piiwashiyit.

Moushoom continued, "My dad pulled over and got out his rifle. 'Come on, my boy, maybe you'll get your first moose,' my dad said ..." Moushoom's voice faded and he stared into the distance. That's how Moushoom looked when he was remembering.

Nolin wiggled in his seat. Finally he asked, "Did you get one?"

Kiiyapit Mooshoom piikishkwew, "Paapaa kii paashkew pi soon fiizii kii ootinum. 'Aashtum moon pchi gaarsoon, apootikweh toon praamyii naariyaanl ka nipahow,' itwew Paapaa." Mooshoom poon piikishkwew pi waayow iitapiw. Aykooshi Mooshoom aen shnaakooshit ka naakatwaytuk.

Nolin mamahtapew piiyish itwew, "Payek chiin ki tawawow?"

"Not so fast, Nooshishim. We followed those tracks into the bush. Finally, we spotted the moose feeding on some willow branches. My dad handed me his gun. I got the moose in my sights and shot him ..."

Nolin waited.

"Kaya kakwayyahoo, Nooshishim. Gii maatahanaan daan li bwaa. Kaytaway gii waapamananihk lii zaariyaanl aen miitishoochik daan lii soohl. Paapaa gii paytshinamaak soon fiizii. Gii itwawow laariyaanl pi gii paashkishwow."

Nolin kii payhoo.

"By the time we gutted the moose, a real big storm had blown in ... a whiteout. We skinned the moose as fast as our frozen hands could go. My dad flipped the moose skin and crawled underneath the furry side. I didn't want to. It looked gross. But I was frozen stiff, so finally I joined him. We pulled that skin around us and waited out the storm."

Nolin shivered and pulled his coat tighter.

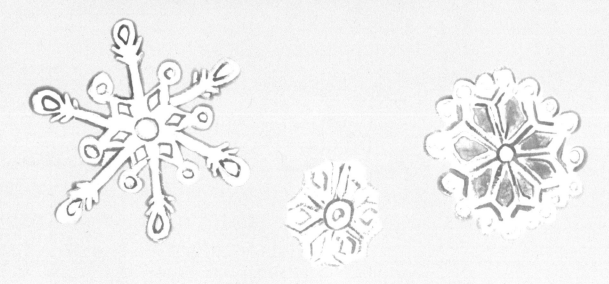

"Ka poon pakoochaynayahk laariyaanl enn groos taanpet ki payamakun ... kishchimachikishikow. Kayshikow gii poon paahkoonikanaan aen shpiishchiyaak aata nutr maen aen akwachiyaak. Paapaa kii apootinew la poo daariyaanl pi ki shaykoo iita li pwel ka ayyak. No niiya ooya. Oooshaam kii mayatun. Gii shiitowachin, dawatch niishta gii shaykoon avik wiiya. Gii wawaykwaninaan la poo pi gi payhounaan chi poonmachikishikaak."

Nolin kii nanikachew pi soon caapoo ki shiishchipitum.

Moushoom chuckled. "That moose skin saved our hides. And that, my boy, is how I got my name. 'Moose...um!' Get it?"

Mooshoom paapew. "La poo daariyaanl gii paashpikoonaan. Aykooshi moon noon 'Moose...um' kaa ayaayaan! Ki nishitootenn chiin?"

Nolin laughed. "As if!"

Soon Moushoom turned off the highway. The streetlights of Meadow Lake glowed through the blowing snow. Nolin's house shimmered with Christmas lights.

Nolin paapew. "Nimoo taapwew!"

Wiipatchikoo Mooshoom ka kweshkiit sur li highway. La klayrtii di la rue ki waapaten aen waashkopayik daan la niigh. Nolin sa mayzoon kii kishchi waashkotew avik lii light di Krismas.

When they stopped, Nolin ran ahead and opened the door. The house was bursting with aunties, uncles and cousins. Laughter and delicious smells filled the air.

Mom hugged him. "Hi, honey. Did you have fun at Moushoom's?"

Before Nolin could answer, Auntie Gigi planted a mushy kiss on his cheek. Then Auntie Vickie's big red lips smacked him on the other cheek. Yuck, he hated kissing!

Ka nakiichik, Nolin ki niikanipatow chi paashtaynuk la porrt. La mayzoon kii mooshkinew avik lii taant, lii zoonk, pi lii koozin. Mishchet paapiwin pi kii myeumakwun aen pashooyen.

Oomaamaawa kii shakikwaynikoo. "Kii moochikanitaan chiin avik Mooshoom?"

Avaan kaykway chii itwayt ashay, sa taant Gigi ka oochaymikoot. Sa taant Vickie wiishta avik sii groos babiin roozh ka oochaymikoot loot sa jhoo. Yuck, no kii miyeutum aen oochaykayt!

Nolin blushed when he saw his cousin peeking around the corner, giggling at him.

Nolin kii mihkoowaypayiw aen paashpapamikoot sa koozinn pi aen pahpiyikoot.

Moushoom hugged his brother, Ol' Uncle Gabe, and then made his way around the room shaking hands and greeting everyone. Auntie Vickie left red lipstick on Moushoom's cheek too. He didn't seem to mind kisses.

Niikaan Mooshoom kii shakikwaynew soon frayr, li vyeu Gabe, pi kii waashakatew la shaambr aen shakishchayniwet pi aen naakishkawat kaakiyow. Ta taant Vickie kii nakatamowew li lipstick roozh Mooshoom sa jhooiyew. Kii miiyeutum aen oochaymikashoot.

The living room looked different. Furniture was pushed aside and a long table filled the space. Nolin breathed in the smells as Mom and the aunties brought plates piled high with food.

"Come and eat," called Mom.

Moushoom sat at the end of the table and motioned for Nolin to sit next to him.

Paakaan la shaambr iita ka kiiwikayk kii shnaakwun. La foornichur kii aahkinikatew paakaan itay. Pi kii mooshkinew avik enn graand taab. Nolin kaakiyow kaykway kii miyatum, omaamaawa pi sa taant ki paytawuk lii zaasyet plaen di maangii.

"Paymiitshook," taypwew Maamaan.

Mooshoom kii apiw oboot la taab pi kii waashtahamwew Nolin chii pay wiitapimikoot.

Mom asked, "Dad, will you say grace?"

Moushoom began, "We're happy to have the family together for the beginning of a new year. Let us give thanks ..." When Moushoom finished, everyone made the sign of the cross.

Mom said, "I want to thank Dad, for giving us the moose meat ..."

Maamaan kii kakwaychimew opaapaawa chi nikaan ayamihayit.

Mooshoom maachitow, "Ni miyeytenaan nutr famii ka naakishkatoochik li zhoor di laan aen maachipayik. Maarsii itwaytaak." Mooshoom ka kiishitaat kakiyow, li siing di la krway ki ooshitawuk.

Maamaan itwew, "Maarsii ditow Paapaa aen kii miikooyaak la vyaand daariyaanl."

Nolin nudged Moushoom, giggling. "Is that the moose from the blizzard?"

"Sh, your mom's still talking," whispered Moushoom.

"... and Bunny, thanks for catching such a big whitefish. Gigi and Vickie, thanks for bringing dessert. Let's dig in!"

Nolin chakawew Mooshoom payshkish aen paahpit, "Aykwaana chiin laaryaanl la taanpett ooschi?"

"Sh, ki Maamaan kiyapit piikishkwew," kiimootchiitwew Mooshoom.

"Maarsii Bunny aen kii kaashchitinut lii groo pwasoon blaan. Maarsii Gigi pi Vickie poor li dessert aen kii paytayaek. Michinshook!"

Nolin filled his plate with moose meat, tourtière, mashed potatoes, gravy, and lii beignes. He ate every bite and asked, "What's for dessert?"

"Saskatoon pie, blueberry pie, and carrot pudding with caramel sauce," replied Auntie Gigi.

Nolin smacked his lips. "Mmm, some of each, please."

Everyone laughed.

Nolin kii mooshkinatow soon naasyet avik la vyaand daariyaanl, lii toortier, lii paataak ka shikwahooshchik, la soos, pi lii beigne. "Kaakiyow kii kitow pi kiyapit kwaychikaymoo poor li dessert?"

"La taart di pwayr, la taart di grenn bleu, pi la poochin di kaarot avik la soos di caramel," itwew ta taant Gigi.

Nolin noohkwatum sii babinn. "Mmm, kakiyow apishiish sil voo play."

Kaakiyow paahpiwuk.

While the aunties stacked dishes and got dessert, Nolin tapped Uncle Bunny's shoulder. "Uncle, did you bring your fiddle?"

"You bet," said Uncle Bunny. "When dinner's finished we'll put the table back and make room to dance."

Maykwat lii taant la visel aen taashikakihk pi li dessert aen naatakihk, Nolin taashikawew daan soon nipooliyew. "Moon nook toon vyaeloon chiin kii paytaan?"

"Taapwey," itwew nook Bunny. "Poonmiitishootwawi la taab kiitwawm ka aashtanaan la plaas chi ooshitayaak poor la daans."

After dinner Nolin helped clean up.

Mom raised her eyebrows at Moushoom. "Dad, whatever you did to my son, thank you. He's never been so eager to help out."

"That's our little surprise," replied Moushoom, flashing a wink at Nolin.

Apray jhinii Nolin kii wiichiyiwew aen paykishchikayit.

Maamaan naykwapamew Mooshoom. "Paapaa taanshi ka tootawut moon gaarsoon, maarsii. Nowiikaatch maana nootay wiishihiwew."

"Niiyanaan piiko gishkaytaynaan," itwew Mooshoom, aen chiipiikweshtawat Nolin.

Uncle Bunny pulled out his fiddle and started tuning it.
SQUEEK SQUAWK SQUEEK SQUAWK!
He rubbed some rosin on the bow and soon music flowed from the fiddle. Ol' Gabe clacked his spoons and Mom strummed her guitar.

Nook Bunny soon vyaeloon kichipitum pi ki maamiinwaa paykahum.
SQUEEK SQUAWK SQUEEK SQUAWK!
Laarkaansyoon ki shinikoonum daan soon naarshett pi wiipachikoo la musuk ka wayupayik soon vyaeloon ooshchi. Li vyeu Gabe sii chooyayr maatawew pi Maamaan soon guitar kitooshchikew.

Uncle Bunny started with a slow tune. Moushoom pulled Auntie Gigi up to waltz. Soon everyone was dancing ... except Nolin. One of the girl cousins asked him to dance, but he got shy. He ducked behind the musicians.

Nolin peeked over Uncle Bunny's shoulder. The fiddle gleamed and the bow sliced up and down. He felt the music seep into his bones. Nolin's toes started to tap.

After several slow dances, Moushoom nodded to Uncle Bunny.

Nook Bunny maachi kitooshchikew nishikat. Mooshoom wiichimooshtawew ta taant Gigi poor enn waltz. Wiiputchikoo kaahkiyow niimiwuk Nolin pikoo. Payek sii koozinn kii kaakwaychimikoo chi niimit maaka ki niipaywooshew. Kii kaashoo aan naaryayr lii musisien.

Nolin paashpapew disseu nook Bunny sii zipool. Li vyaeloon kii waashishkoopayin pi laarshet taapishkoot kaykway aen maanishamihk aen shinakwuhk. La musuk mooshitow daan sii zoo. Nolin avik sii zaartay taypwayshkum la musuk.

Apray mishchet lii daans plu laan Mooshoom nanamishkwayyiishtawew nook Bunny.

Uncle Bunny broke into the rollicking rhythm of the "Red River Jig."

Moushoom, the aunties, the uncles, and the cousins jigged to the beat.

Moushoom motioned to Nolin. "Áshtum óta, Nooshishim."

Nolin's feet froze. What if he couldn't remember the steps? He wished he could disappear under the moosehide from Moushoom's story.

Nook Bunny kaytaway ka maachi kitooshchiket "la jig di la Rivyar Roozh."

Mooshoom, lii taant, lii zoonk, pi lii koozin la jig shooshkwaypinikaywuk.

Mooshoom itwew, "Aashtum oota Nooshishim."

Nolin taapishkoot sii pyii aen aakwatinyiik. Kaykway kiishpin waanikaychi sii stepp? Kii nootay kaashoo aansoor mooshoon sa poo daariyaanl taapishkoot Mooshoom ka atayookayt.

Moushoom took off his sash and lassoed Nolin, pulling him onto the floor. He quickly wrapped the sash around Nolin's waist.

Nolin started hesitantly with the basic step, but the music made him go faster. He watched his grandpa's feet and copied what he did. Panting for breath, Moushoom bowed out. When the tempo changed, Nolin stepped to the rhythm. He felt the dancing in his bones. All by himself he did the "cross step," then the "bunny step," then the "Chi Galop."

Mooshoom kaychikoonum sa saenchur flayshii pi kii taypikwatew Nolinwa, wiikoopitew taykay li plaanshii. Kii wawaykinew avik sa saenchur flayshii.

Nolin kii shiitaytum niikaan maaka nawutch kakwayahoo aen chiikitak la musuk. Pishkapatamwew Mooshoom sii pyii pi kii naashpihtotawew. Aen kipaatatuk Mooshoom pooni nimew. Ka mayshkochipayik Nolin ki taapweshkum. Kii mooshihoo la musuk daan si zoo. Kii payako nimew "la daans di balay," "la daans di lyavr," pi li "Pchi Galoo."

By this time everyone was clapping in a circle around him. What other step could he show? He imitated the funny dance Moushoom had done when he took the bannock from the oven.

"Hey, that's the 'Bannock Jig!'" Moushoom yelled.

Everyone laughed.

Kaahkiyow leu maen pakamahamwuk pi aen roond ki ooshitawuk pi ki waashakashkawaywuk. Kaykway paakaan aykwa chi niimit. Kii naashpitootawew Mooshoom ka kii niimiyit sa gallet ka kitinat daan li pwel ooshchi.

"Hey," Mooshoom taypwew, "'la jig di gallet' ka niimiyen!"

Kaahkiyow paapiwuk.

When the music stopped, Mom gave him a big bear hug. "I'm so proud of you, my boy. You dance just like your Moushoom."

Nolin grinned. "Moushoom's right, Mom. I've got dancing in my bones."

Mom kissed Nolin's forehead. He didn't mind this kiss. He felt her love tingle down his body. "Hey," he thought. "I've got love in my bones, too."

Ka poonipayik la musuk Maamaan kischi shaakikwaynikoo taapishkoot aen noor. "Ki kischitaymitin moon gaarsoon. Taapishkoot ki Mooshoom aenshinimiiyen."

Nolin papinakooshew. "Mooshoom taapwew Maamaan. La daans aashtew daan mii zoo."

Maamaan oochaymew Nolin daan soon frooniyik. Kii miyeytum aen oochaymikashoot. Kii mooshitow aen shakiihikashoot daan soo korr. "Hey" itaytum, "niishta lamoor daan mii zoo daayaan."

Glossary:

Áshtum óta: "Come here" in the Michif Language.

Beignes: fried bread; a kind of bannock.

Cutline: a pathway cleared through a wooded area.

Michif: some Métis people call themselves Michif, rather than Métis.

Midnight Lake: a village in Saskatchewan, at the southern end of the boreal forest, 80 km south of Meadow Lake.

Moushoom: "grandfather" in the Michif Language.

Nolin: Métis surname, now used as a given name.

Nooshishim: "my grandson" in the Michif Language.

Oyhoy!: Yikes!

Tourtière: meat pie.

Tourtière:

½ lb/¼ kg ground beef
½ lb/¼ kg lean ground pork
¾ cup/175 ml potato water
¾ cup/175 ml mashed potatoes
1 onion chopped
Salt to taste
¼ tsp/1.25 ml each cloves and sage
½ tsp/2.5 ml allspice

Dough:
1 ½ cup/375 ml flour
4 tbsp/60 ml lard
¾ cup/175 ml milk
4 tbsp/60 ml baking powder
¾ tsp/3.75 ml salt

Add potato water to meat and onion. Cook until
meat turns grey in colour. Add mashed potatoes and
seasoning. Prepare dough in usual way. Line pie plate
with dough. Fill with meat mixture and cover with
crust. Cut slits on top of crust to let out steam. Bake
at 350°F/180°C for ½ hour or until crust is golden
brown.

Recipe by Rose Fleury.

The Creative Team:

Wilfred Burton grew up north of Glaslyn in the Midnight Lake area of Saskatchewan. His mother passed on her love of fiddle music and dance to all of her children. The minute Don Messer was heard on the radio, the family would begin to dance. The richness of growing up at that time is the basis for the stories he now shares. Even though this book is a work of fiction, there are "real" characters and events from Wilfred's life throughout the story. He currently dances with the Riel Reelers, and continues to teach dance to students young and old.

Since 1979, Wilfred has been a teacher in La Loche and Regina, Saskatchewan. He has worked mostly in elementary schools. He also taught for several years at the Saskatchewan Urban Native Teacher Education Program, University of Regina, working with Aboriginal pre-service teachers. He is currently the Differentiated Learning Consultant for Regina Public Schools.

This is his second collaborative writing effort with his friend, Anne Patton. The first collaboration, *Fiddle Dancer*, was nominated in three categories at the Saskatchewan Book Awards, was nominated at the Ânskohk Aboriginal Literature Festival and Book Awards, and is a 2009 nominee for the Shining Willow category for the Saskatchewan Young Readers' Choice Award. Despite these accolades, Wilfred's reward is the close collaboration on a creative endeavor with a friend.

Anne Patton grew up in the Niagara Peninsula in southern Ontario. After moving to Saskatchewan, she taught elementary school (kindergarten, special education, primary, and middle years) for many years. While teaching, Anne was frustrated by the scarcity of children's literature reflecting life in Saskatchewan. She promised herself that she would write children's books when she had more leisure time. After retiring, she worked at the Saskatchewan Urban Native Teacher Education Program instructing Aboriginal pre-service teachers. At the same time, Anne launched her writing career.

Anne's first five books are part of *Scholastic's Literacy Place*. For several years, she has collaborated with her friend Wilfred Burton on this series about a Métis boy who learns to jig. This book is the second in the series. Anne has also written a children's novel, to be published in 2010, about the Barr Colonists who founded Lloydminster, Alberta/Saskatchewan. She is now a full-time Nanna who makes frequent trips to Calgary and Victoria to read stories to her grandchildren. Anne loves gardening, camping, and having adventures of all kinds.

Norman Fleury, originally from St. Lazare, Manitoba, is a gifted Michif storyteller. He grew up in a traditional Michif home and community. He is a fluent Michif speaker, and can speak several other Aboriginal languages such as Cree, Ojibwa, and Dakota, as well as French and English. He has worked extremely hard in the promotion and preservation of Michif, including the production of language resources and an introductory Michif dictionary, as well as giving workshops at many different gatherings such as Back to Batoche Days, Métis Days, and National Aboriginal Day celebrations.

Norman went to Brandon University, and he also enrolled as a life skills instructor trainer. He later worked as a university administrative coordinator in charge of student affairs, and served as a community liaison. He worked in corrections in Brandon, and also worked in group homes. In the past, he worked as the executive director of the Brandon Indian and Métis Friendship Centre.

Norman was chosen by the Métis community to be an Elder at Brandon University. For the past twenty years, he has been farming near Woodnorth, Manitoba, while working for the Manitoba Métis Federation (MMF) as its Michif Language Program Director. He has been active with the MMF since 1967. He also held local MMF chairperson positions in St. Lazare, Rivers and Brandon. Norman presently lives at his farm near Woodnorth with his wife, Ruth-Anne and his children, Chantelle and Mark. His 107-year old mother, Flora Fleury (née Leclerc), has been his greatest inspiration. With this inspiration, Norman continues to passionately share his Michif culture and language.

Sherry Farrell Racette is one of the early builders of the Gabriel Dumont Institute (GDI). During her tenure with GDI—as an educator, author, and illustrator—Sherry has left an endurable legacy of highly-acclaimed resources including *The Flower Beadwork People*, *The Flags of the Métis*, and several posters, and most recently, *Fiddle Dancer* and *Better that Way*, both of which were nominated for Saskatchewan Book Awards. She has also illustrated Maria Campbell's *Stories of the Road Allowance People* and Freda Ahenakew's *Wisahkecahk Flies to the Moon*.

In addition to illustration, Sherry's art practice includes painting, beadwork, and textiles. In 2009-10, she will be the Anne Ray Fellow at the School of Advanced Research in Santa Fe, New Mexico, and following that she will take up a cross-appointment in the Departments of Native Studies and Women and Gender Studies at the University of Manitoba.